# The Ballad of Stinky Pete the Pirate

## Story and Art by Tao Blaine Baker ☸ Colors by Jeremy Havlick

### For LeAnn ~

You are my morning star. Thank you for going on this journey with me. - T

*The Ballad of Stinky Pete the Pirate*. Copyright © 2008 by Tao Blaine Baker

Library of Congress Cataloging-in-Publication Data

Baker, Tao Blaine, 1962 -
The Ballad of Stinky Pete the Pirate / [Tao Blaine Baker]
p.  cm.

Stinky Pete was a Pirate as a matter of fact,

But personal hygiene was something he lacked.

He was offensive to all pirates the small and the stout,

He even made his parrot's feathers fall out.

He would sit all alone when they ate all their grub,

He felt like a loser, he felt like a schlub.

The crew thought about making ol' Pete walk the plank,

They were so very tired of the way that he stank!

Stinky Pete had no friends...he was always morose,

It wasn't his fault that he always smelled gross!

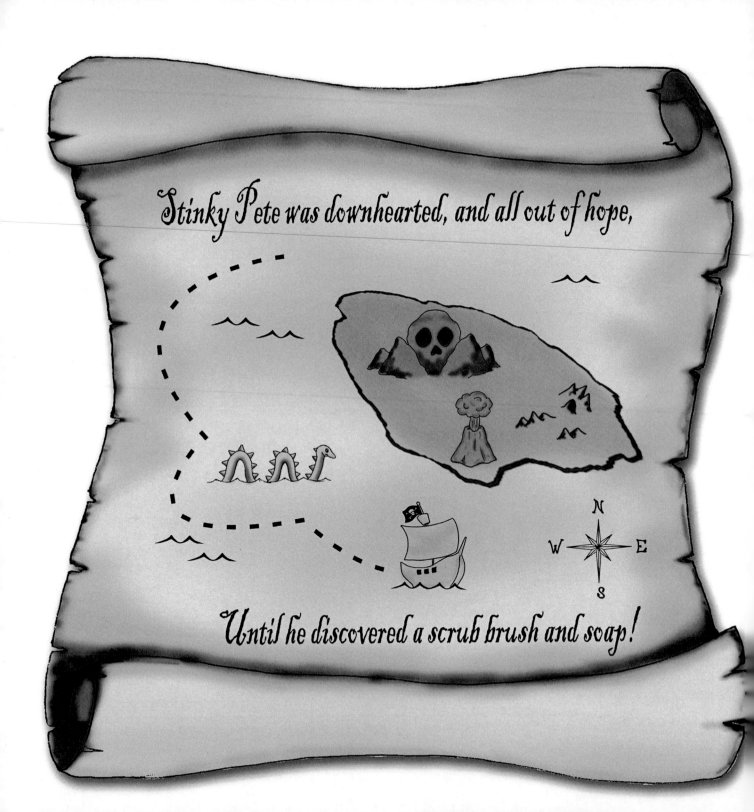

Stinky Pete was downhearted, and all out of hope,

Until he discovered a scrub brush and soap!

He washed all his fingers,

He washed 'tween his toes...

He was clean as a whistle, the pirates let out a roar,

For Stinky Pete the pirate,

W as stinky no more!!!

The Moral of this story is, "just do the math...

If you don't have any friends just go take a bath."

The End